PUFFIN BOOKS

GRISELDA F.G.M.

There are all sorts of people who need the help of Griselda, the fairy-godmother with a difference. Her spells don't always work out as planned, but with the help of her multi-coloured mouse Samuel, she gets there in the end.

Her good deeds include rescuing Prince Popoff from his three great-aunts and whizzing him off to the circus for a bit of fun; solving the mystery of the bread which just won't rise; trying to help Mrs Rubadub with her spring-cleaning and helping Harmony Honeysuckle regain her voice in time for the concert.

Griselda zooms around with Samuel, solving problems and creating chaos. Children will enjoy this fun magical story as they follow Griselda's unpredictable adventures.

Margaret Ryan was born in Paisley in Scotland and now lives in Greenock with her husband. She has two children and was a teacher before she became a writer full-time.

GRISELDA F.G.M.

Margaret Ryan

Illustrated by John Eastwood

To Fiona
Best Wishes
Margaret Ryan
31/1/95.

PUFFIN BOOKS

PUFFIN BOOKS

Published by the Penguin Group
Penguin Books Ltd, 27 Wrights Lane, London W8 5TZ, England
Penguin Books USA Inc., 375 Hudson Street, New York, New York 10014, USA
Penguin Books Australia Ltd, Ringwood, Victoria, Australia
Penguin Books Canada Ltd, 10 Alcorn Avenue, Toronto, Ontario, Canada M4V 3B2
Penguin Books (NZ) Ltd, 182–190 Wairau Road, Auckland 10, New Zealand

Penguin Books Ltd, Registered Offices: Harmondsworth, Middlesex, England

First published by Blackie and Son Ltd 1991
Published in Puffin Books 1993
3 5 7 9 10 8 6 4 2

Text copyright © Margaret Ryan, 1991
Illustrations copyright © John Eastwood, 1991
All rights reserved

The moral right of the author has been asserted

Printed in England by Clays Ltd, St Ives plc
Filmset in Plantin

1 Griselda FGM

Griselda, the fairy-godmother, was sitting by the fire, trying to mend a large hole in the left knee of her best pair of blue jeans.

'Maybe I should have that high garden hedge round the cottage cut down instead of trying to whizz through it,' she said to Samuel, her multi-coloured mouse. 'I really don't know what's wrong with that spell.'

Samuel snored loudly in reply. He was curled up inside an old furry slipper, sleeping off his lunch.

Just then the alarm on Griselda's
micro-chipped and scratched super fairy-

godmother watch went BLEEP BLEEP.

'Ah,' she said. 'Time to look through the magic window, and see who needs my help today.'

Samuel immediately wakened up, and leapt out of the slipper. He liked looking through the magic window. He ran up Griselda's arm and onto her shoulder.

Griselda went over to the cottage window. It was divided into six panes of glass, five clear, and one cloudy. Griselda blew gently on the cloudy one, then rubbed it with her sleeve. Slowly a picture began to appear . . .

'Why, it's little Prince Popoff,' said Griselda. 'I wonder why he needs my help today.'

Little Prince Popoff was sitting at the table in the palace dining-room with his three great-aunts; great-aunt Niggle, great-aunt Naggle and great-aunt Mona. They had come to look after him while the king and queen were off on a tour of the kingdom.

Great-aunt Niggle had a long long nose which reached nearly down to her chin. Great-aunt Naggle had a long long chin which reached nearly down to her chest. And great-aunt Mona wore long long cardigans which she knitted herself. They all had long long tongues, and Griselda and Samuel listened to them using them . . .

'Don't forget to use your napkin, Popoff, and don't speak with your mouth full,' said great-aunt Niggle.

'Don't forget to drink your milk, Popoff, and eat up all your greens,' said great-aunt Naggle.

'Why aren't you wearing that lovely purple cardigan with the green and

orange stripes it took me ages to knit you,
Popoff?' said great-aunt Mona.

'Oh dear, dear,' said Griselda sucking in her cheeks, and shaking her head. 'I think I'd better whizz off to the palace, and take little Prince Popoff out for a bit of fun. Are you coming, Samuel?'

Samuel blew out his cheeks and nodded his head. 'I suppose I'd better come and keep an eye on you,' he said. Then he grabbed a strand of Griselda's long fair hair, swung on the end of it, and plopped into the pocket of her T-shirt. The pocket was the safest place to be when whizzing about with Griselda.

While Samuel held on tight, and prepared himself for take-off, Griselda did a little disco dance on the carpet, then said the magic words; TIME TO BE OFF TO THE PALACE. And they were off, whizzing through the air with a *WHISH*, a *WHOOSH* and a *WHIRL* . . .

And before you could say ANCIENT OLD

AUNTIES, they had landed in the palace dining-room. In the middle of the table. In the middle of the custard.

'Oops, sorry everyone,' said Griselda, stepping out of the bowl and leaving yellow footprints all over the white table-cloth. 'I'm not very good at landings.'

'You can say that again,' muttered Samuel from the depths of her T-shirt pocket.

Little Prince Popoff was delighted to see them, and jumped up from the table. 'Hi there, Griselda. Hi there, Samuel. Great to see you.' He didn't mind about Griselda's splashdown in the custard. He didn't like custard anyway.

Great-aunt Niggle liked custard, though. But not dripping down her long long nose. She wiped the drips off with her napkin. 'Why can't you use the front door like everyone else, Griselda?'

she said.

Great-aunt Naggle liked custard too. But not dribbling down her long long chin. She wiped the dribbles off with her napkin. 'Why can't you learn to land properly, Griselda?' she said.

Great-aunt Mona liked custard over everything, even chips. But not all over her long long cardigan that she'd knitted herself. She tried to wipe the splashes off

12

with her napkin. 'I'll never get the custard stains out of this cardigan, Griselda,' she said.

'I really am sorry,' said Griselda. 'I just came by to take Popoff out for the afternoon, but I'll do a little spell and clean up the mess before I go.' And before anyone could stop her, she did a little disco dance on the carpet, closed her eyes and said the magic words:

ROSES ARE RED

VIOLETS ARE BLUE

PLEASE CLEAN UP THIS MESS

AND THE OLD AUNTIES TOO.

There was a *FIZZ*, a *THUMP* and a *BANG*, and the table was immediately covered in big fat soapy suds. So were the great aunts. They started yelling . . . 'OWL YOWL WOWL . . .'

Samuel groaned. 'You're not very good at spelling either, Griselda. I think it's time we left.'

And they did. Griselda, Samuel and Popoff whizzed off with a *WHISH*, a *WHOOSH*, a *WHIRL* and the magic words . . . TIME TO BE OFF TO THE CIRCUS . . . because that was Prince Popoff's favourite place.

They landed in the big top. In the middle of the ring. In the middle of the elephants.

'Oops sorry, elephants,' said Griselda dodging round the trunks. 'I'm not very good at landings.'

But Prince Popoff thought it was all great fun, though Samuel wasn't quite so sure. Elephants are rather big up close if you're a mouse.

Then the ring-master, Mr Maxter, hurried forward. 'Ah, Prince Popoff, Griselda, little Samuel,' he said. 'How nice to see you. Come, take a ringside seat,

the show is just beginning. You will see it all, except for the high wire act who cannot perform because of their terrible colds.'

'Oh dear. What a shame,' said Griselda. Then she had an idea, and whispered it to the ring-master.

'I think that's a splendid idea,' said Mr

Maxter.

'I think it's a rotten idea,' said Samuel who was close enough to hear.

Then they sat down to watch the show, and little Prince Popoff had a wonderful time. He gasped at the jugglers, cheered at the chimps, and fell about laughing when the clowns threw a bucket of water over him that turned into confetti.

Then the ring-master made a special announcement. 'I'm sorry to have to tell you that the high wire act, *The Great Geneezes*, will not be able to perform because they have got *The Great Sneezes*. But instead I have another very special high wire act for you. None other than *The Amazing Prince Popoff with Griselda his Fairy-Godmother and Samuel the Multi-Coloured Mouse*.

'Oh wow,' said Prince Popoff. 'Do you think we can really do the high wire act?'

'With a little help from my magic, we can,' laughed Griselda.

Samuel shook his head, and crossed his claws, his ears and his eyes.

To the cheers of the crowd, they walked into the ring, and started to climb up the long long ladder.

'It's a long long way up,' said Prince Popoff.

'It's a long long way down,' muttered Samuel.

But, for once, Griselda got the magic right, and she whished and whooshed and whirled them through the air with the greatest of ease, even landing them safely in the middle of the ring at the end. The audience loved the act and clapped and cheered.

'You can come and be in my show anytime,' said Mr Maxter after the performance, and he gave Prince Popoff four

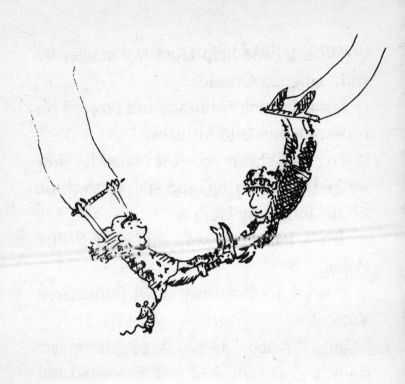

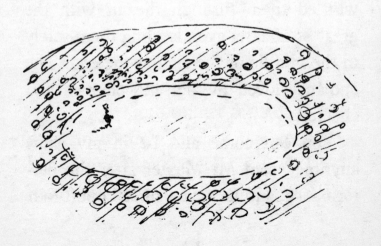

free tickets. 'Bring your great-aunties,' he said.

Then they all whizzed off home.

Back at the palace, little Prince Popoff said, 'Thank you for a great afternoon, Griselda. I had a magic time.'

'So did I,' said Griselda, and she was so pleased with herself for getting all the magic at the circus right, that she decided to try the magic words again that would whizz her safely through her garden hedge. Samuel crouched down in her pocket, closed his eyes, and covered his head with his claws.

ROSES ARE RED

VIOLETS ARE BLUE

LOOK OUT GARDEN HEDGE

I'M COMING THROUGH.

Griselda and Samuel whizzed off with a *WHISH*, a *WHOOSH*, a *WHIRL*, and a *RRRRIIIIPPPP* . . . They were back

19

in the cottage, but Griselda's best blue jeans now had a large hole in the right knee.

'That's not supposed to happen, Samuel,' she said. 'I wonder what I'm doing wrong . . . I'll have to try to sew up the hole in that knee tomorrow, but I've just run out of blue thread, I'll have to use pink wool instead.'

2   Griselda Bakes Some Bread

Griselda, the fairy-godmother, was sitting in the garden of her cottage, trying to mend the large hole in the right knee of her best pair of blue jeans, with pink wool.

'Ouch,' she said, as she missed the

material and poked the darning needle into her knee instead. 'That prickly hedge is to blame for the state of these jeans, Samuel. Do you think I should dig it out and plant a fence instead?'

But Samuel, her multi-coloured mouse, wasn't listening, and snored and whistled in reply. He was curled up inside an old kettle Griselda had put out in the garden for the robins to nest in.

Just then the alarm on Griselda's micro-chipped and scratched super fairy-godmother watch went TWEET TWEET. Griselda banged it off a tree until it went BLEEP BLEEP.

'Ah,' said Griselda. 'Time to look through the magic window, and see who needs my help today.'

Samuel immediately wakened up, and leapt out of the old kettle. He liked looking through the magic window. He

ran up Griselda's arm and onto her shoulder.

Griselda went over to the cottage window. It was divided into six panes of glass, five clear and one cloudy. Griselda blew gently on the cloudy one, then rubbed it with her sleeve. Slowly a picture began to appear . . .

'Why it's Mr Yumtumski, the baker,' said Griselda. 'I wonder why he needs my help today?'

Mr Yumtumski was in the bakehouse

at the back of his shop, taking loaves out of the big oven. He looked at the loaves, and gave a loud yell. 'Crumbly crumpets,' he cried, taking off his tall white hat and jumping on it. 'Just look at these loaves.

They look like pancakes. Flat, flat pancakes. Why don't the loaves rise today? Are they too tired? Are they too lazy? Don't they want to be eaten?'

Jani, the baker's boy turned bright red and said, 'Oh dear, Mr Yumtumski, I think I forgot . . .'

But Mr Yumtumski wasn't listening. 'Forty years I have been baking bread,' he said. 'Forty years and I have never had loaves like this . . .'

'Oh dear, Mr Yumtumski,' Jani tried again. 'I think I forgot to . . .'

But Mr Yumtumski still wasn't listening. He put one last loaf into the oven. 'Forty years,' he said, 'and all I can bake are loaves you could slide under a door.'

'Oh dear dear,' said Griselda sucking in her cheeks and shaking her head. 'I think I'd better whizz off to the bakery

and help out Mr Yumtumski. Are you coming, Samuel?'

Samuel blew out his cheeks and nodded his head. 'I suppose I'd better come in case you do any half-baked spells,' he said. Then he grabbed a strand of Griselda's long fair hair, swung on the end of it, and plopped into the pocket of her T-shirt. The pocket was the safest place to be when whizzing about with Griselda.

While Samuel held on tight, and prepared himself for take-off, Griselda did a little disco dance on the carpet, then said the magic words. TIME TO BE OFF TO THE BAKERY. And they were off whizzing through the air with a *WHISH*, a *WHOOSH* and a *WHIRL*. And before you could say, MOULDY OLD MUFFINS, they had landed in the bakery. In the middle of the table. In the middle of the meringues.

'Oops sorry, everyone,' said Griselda, crunching through the cakes, and leaving a trail of broken meringues everywhere. 'I'm not very good at landings.'

Samuel peeped out from her pocket. 'But I'm good at eating meringues,' he said. 'I'll just help you clear up, Mr Yumtumski.' And he helped to clear bits of meringue straight into his mouth.

Mr Yumtumski sighed.

27

'Griselda,' he said. 'You know you are my favourite fairy-godmother, but why can't you use the shop door like everyone else?'

'I really am sorry, Mr Yumtumski,' said Griselda. 'I just came by to help you with your flat loaves, but I'll do a little spell and fix the meringues first.'

And before anyone could stop her, she did a little disco dance on the tiled floor, closed her eyes and said the magic words.

ROSES ARE RED

VIOLETS ARE BLUE

MAKE THE BASHED UP MERINGUES

AS GOOD AS NEW.

There was a *FIZZ*, a *THUMP* and a *BANG*, and the bits of meringue were all joined together. With sticking plaster. Even Samuel had a large piece over his mouth.

'I suppose you think that's funny,' he

squeaked, peeling off the plaster and smoothing out his whiskers.

'Sorry,' said Griselda.

'Now you have made things even worse,' said Mr Yumtumski. 'Now I have no loaves and no meringues to sell.'

'Don't worry, Mr Yumtumski,' said Griselda. 'I'll think of something. Perhaps there's a problem with the yeast that makes the loaves rise. I'll do a spell that will make it work better.'

And before anyone could stop her, she did another little disco dance on the tiled floor and said the magic words.

ROSES ARE RED

MY NOSE IS TOO

LOAF IN THE OVEN

RISE UP. PLEASE DO.

There was a *FIZZ*, a *THUMP* and a *BANG* and the oven door flew open. Inside was an enormous loaf which grew and grew and grew. It grew out of the oven and onto the floor. It grew up from the floor and out to the door.

Mr Yumtumski stood looking at it with his arms open wide. Jani stood looking at it with his eyes open wide. Samuel stood looking at it with his mouth open wide ready to eat a bit. Then the enormous loaf squashed him against the bakehouse door, and he had to nip into the keyhole for safety.

'Griselda,' he yelled from his hiding-place. 'Don't just stand there, loafing around. Do something.'

'Hmm? Oh right,' said Griselda, who was just wondering how many toast soldiers the enormous loaf would make. 'I'll say the magic word.' And she did. She said 'STOP'.

And the enormous loaf stopped growing.

At that moment, there was a great noise from outside. Mr Yumtumski squeezed past the loaf and looked out. There were lots of people in his shop all waiting to buy bread.

'We smelled an even more delicious smell than usual,' they said when they saw the baker. 'Can we buy extra bread?'

'Certainly,' Mr Yumtumski beamed. 'But the shape of the bread is a little unusual today, so I will cut you two pieces for the price of one, no?'

'Yes,' everybody agreed.

Griselda smiled and helped to serve all the customers. Samuel smiled and ate up all the crumbs.

When all the bread was sold, Mr Yumtumski said. 'Thank you very much for your help, Griselda. But I still don't know why my loaves came out as flat as pancakes.'

Jani the baker's boy blushed. 'I tried to tell you, Mr Yumtumski,' he said. 'I think I forgot to put the yeast into the mixture.'

'Oh was that all?' said Mr Yumtumski and gave a great laugh that could be heard for miles around and Samuel and Griselda and Jani joined in.

And Griselda was so pleased with herself at getting the magic nearly right that she decided to try the magic words that would whizz her safely through her garden hedge. Samuel crouched down in her pocket, closed his eyes and covered his head with his claws.

ROSES ARE RED

VIOLETS ARE BLUE

NICE GARDEN HEDGE

I'M COMING THROUGH.

Griselda and Samuel whizzed off with a *WHISH*, a *WHOOSH*, a *WHIRL* and a *RRRRRIIIIIPPPPP* . . . They were back in the cottage, but Griselda's best blue jeans now had a large tear in the left pocket.

'That's definitely not supposed to happen, Samuel,' she said. 'I wonder what I'm doing wrong . . . I'll have to try to sew up the tear in that pocket tomorrow, but now I've run out of pink wool. I'll just have to use green garden twine instead.'

3   Griselda the Police Person

Griselda, the fairy-godmother, was lying on the floor with her legs up on a chair, trying to mend the tear in the left pocket of her best pair of blue jeans with green garden twine.

'These won't be my best blue jeans much longer,' she said to Samuel, her multi-coloured mouse, 'if I don't get that hedge spell right. What do you think I'm doing wrong?'

'Zzzzz wheeee burble,' snored Samuel from his sleeping place among the hairy peaches in the fruit bowl.

'No, I don't think that's part of the spell, Samuel,' said Griselda as she tried to get her head down to her pocket to bite off the green garden twine.

Samuel opened one lazy eye, and looked at her. 'Is that some new kind of keep fit?' he asked.

Before Griselda could reply, the alarm on her micro-chipped and scratched super fairy-godmother watch went DING DONG. Griselda thumped it on the floor till it went BLEEP BLEEP.

'Ah,' she said. 'Time to look through the magic window to see who needs my help today.'

Samuel immediately opened both eyes and leapt out of the fruit bowl. He liked looking through the magic window. He ran up Griselda's arm and onto her shoulder.

Griselda went over to the cottage window. It was divided into six panes of glass, five clear and one cloudy. Griselda blew gently on the cloudy one, then rubbed it with her sleeve. Slowly a picture began to appear . . .

'Why it's PC Bunion,' said Griselda. 'I wonder why he needs my help today.'

PC Bunion was standing at the village crossroads directing the lunch-time traffic.

'Get along there,' he said to Miss Gossip on her tricycle. 'Can't you pedal any faster?'

'You'll be done for dangerous driving with that pram,' he said to Mrs Smith with her new baby.

'Don't dawdle,' he said to Farmer Charmer with his herd of cows. 'Can't you make these cows MOOOOOVE any faster?'

'Oh dear dear,' said Griselda, sucking in her cheeks, and shaking her head. 'PC Bunion is in a bad mood today. I think I'd better whizz off to the crossroads and see what I can do to help. Are you

coming, Samuel?'

Samuel blew out his cheeks and

nodded his head. 'I'd better come in case you get arrested,' he said. Then he grabbed a strand of Griselda's long fair hair, swung on the end of it, and plopped into her T-shirt pocket. The pocket was the safest place to be when whizzing about with Griselda.

While Samuel held on tight and prepared for take-off, Griselda did a little disco dance on the carpet, then said the magic words: TIME TO BE OFF TO THE CROSSROADS. And they were off, whizzing through the air with a *WHISH*, a *WHOOSH* and a *WHIRL*. And before you could say SILLY OLD COPPERS they had landed at the crossroads. In the middle of the road. In the middle of the cows.

'Oops, sorry everyone,' said Griselda, dodging in and out among the cows. 'I'm not very good at landings.'

'Do hurry along there, Griselda,' said PC Bunion. 'You're getting in the way.'

'Sorry PC Bunion,' said Griselda. 'I just came to see if I could help. You do seem to be very cross today.'

'Perhaps it's because he's on duty at the *cross*roads,' giggled Samuel, peeping out of the T-shirt pocket.

PC Bunion looked stern. 'That's a T-*shirt* pocket you're in, Samuel Mouse,' he said. 'Not a T-*hee* one . . . But it was good of you to come, Griselda. Though I wish you would use the pavement like everyone else. And you're right, I am cross today, but it's all the fault of these

new boots. They're hurting my corns something awful.'

'What a shame,' said Griselda. 'But never mind, I'll do a spell and soon fix that.' And before anyone could stop her, she did a little disco dance on the pavement, closed her eyes and said the magic words.

ROSES ARE RED
VIOLETS ARE BLUE
BRING SOMETHING MORE COMFY
THAN BOOTS THAT ARE NEW.

There was a *FIZZ*, a *THUMP* and a *BANG*, and PC Bunion's new boots dis-

trouble at home. I had completely forgotten it was Mrs Bunion's birthday today, and she was really cross with me till she saw the slippers. They fitted her perfectly, and I'm back in my old comfortable boots again.'

Griselda gave PC Bunion a big smile, and she was so delighted at how well everything had turned out that she decided to try the magic words again that would whizz her safely through her garden hedge. Samuel crouched down in her pocket, closed his eyes and covered his head with his claws.

ROSES ARE RED

VIOLETS ARE BLUE

VERY NICE GARDEN HEDGE

I'M COMING THROUGH

Griselda and Samuel whizzed off with a *WHISH*, a *WHOOSH*, a *WHIRL* and a *RRRRRRRIIIIIIPPPPP* . . . They

were back in the cottage, but Griselda's best blue jeans now had a tear in the right pocket.

'That's absolutely definitely not supposed to happen, Samuel,' she said. 'I wonder what I'm doing wrong . . . I'll have to try to sew up the tear in that pocket tomorrow, but now I've run out of green garden twine. I'll just have to use some white shoe-laces instead.'

4   Griselda and the Spring Cleaning

Griselda, the fairy-godmother, was propped up against the kitchen wall, balanced on one leg, with her tongue sticking out. She was trying to mend the tear in the right pocket of her best pair of blue jeans with white shoe-laces.

'My best pair of blue jeans are beginning to look a bit tattered, Samuel,' she said. 'I wish I could remember how to do that hedge spell properly.'

Samuel snored, sneezed and burped in reply. He was tucked up inside an empty biscuit tin which had been full when he'd found it.

Just then the alarm on Griselda's micro-chipped and scratched super fairy-godmother watch went CUCKOO CUCKOO. Griselda banged it off the wall so it went BLEEP BLEEP.

'Ah,' she said. 'Time to look through the magic window, and see who needs my help today.'

Samuel immediately wakened up, and leapt out of the biscuit tin. He liked looking through the magic window. He ran up Griselda's arm and onto her shoulder.

Griselda went over to the cottage window. It was divided into six panes of glass, five clear and one cloudy. She blew gently on the cloudy one, then rubbed it with her sleeve. Slowly a picture began to appear . . .

'Why it's old Mrs Rubadub,' said Griselda. 'I hardly recognised her without her glasses. I wonder why she needs my help today.'

Old Mrs Rubadub was wearing her pink flowery overall, her pink flowery headscarf, and a worried frown.

'Now where did I put my feather duster?' she muttered. 'I can't start my spring-cleaning without my feather duster. I'm sure I had it a minute ago.'

She searched about till she found it, in among the sweet-williams in the vase on the window ledge. 'I don't remember putting that there,' she said. 'Now where did I put my round tin of wax polish?' She searched about till she found it, propping up the wobbly leg on the fireside chair. 'I don't remember putting that there,' she said. 'Now where did I put my hairy mop? Oh here it is.' And she tried to pick it up, but it wouldn't move, and gave a noisy bark instead.

'Oh it's you, Percy,' said Mrs Rubadub to her Old English sheep-dog. 'I didn't recognise you without my glasses. You haven't seen my hairy mop anywhere, have you? I'll never get on with this spring-cleaning if I don't find it.'

'Oh dear, dear,' said Griselda, sucking in her cheeks and shaking her head. 'Looks like I'd better whizz over there and help Mrs Rubadub with her spring-cleaning. Are you coming, Samuel?'

Samuel blew out his cheeks and nodded his head. 'I'd better come and make sure you don't get swept under the carpet,' he said. Then he grabbed a strand of Griselda's long fair hair, swung on the end of it, and plopped into the pocket of her T-shirt. The pocket was the safest place to be when whizzing about with Griselda. While Samuel held on tight and prepared himself for take-off, Griselda did a little disco dance on the carpet, then said the magic words; TIME TO BE OFF TO MRS RUBADUB'S.

And they were off, whizzing through the air with a *WHISH*, a *WHOOSH* and a *WHIRL*. And before you could say CRUMMY OLD CARPETS, they had landed in the cottage. In the middle of the sink. In the middle of the washing-up water.

'Oops sorry, everyone,' said Griselda, shaking out her trainers and flicking water everywhere. 'I'm not very good at landings.'

'Hullo, postman,' said Mrs Rubadub. 'Have you got a letter for me? I'm afraid I won't be able to read it very well. You see I've lost my glasses.'

'It's not the postman, Mrs Rubadub. It's me, Griselda. Samuel and I have come to help you with your spring-cleaning.'

'Oh it's you, Griselda, and little

Samuel. How nice to see you, or it would be if I could. I should have known it wasn't the postman when you suddenly arrived in the sink. The postman usually comes to the front door.'

'Now where shall I start,' asked Griselda, looking around. 'What would you like cleaned first?'

'Well, the kitchen floor needs doing,' said Mrs Rubadub. 'If only I could find the mop.'

'Don't worry about that,' said Griselda. 'I'll magic you up a mop in no time.' And before anyone could stop her, she did a little disco dance on the linoleum and said the magic words.

ROSES ARE RED

VIOLETS ARE BLUE

HERE COMES A FLOPPY TOP

MOP HEAD FOR YOU

There was a *FIZZ*, a *THUMP* and a

BANG, and Jani, the baker's boy with his floppy top, mop head haircut stood there, dropping little bits of sticky dough all over the floor, and looking very surprised.

'Oops, sorry, Jani,' said Griselda.

'You're not the kind of floppy top, mop head I was looking for.' And Jani went back to the bakery leaving great floury footprints all over the kitchen floor.

'I am sorry, Mrs Rubadub,' said Griselda. 'I don't know what went wrong with that spell. But I tell you what, I'll just get a pail and a scrubbing brush and I'll have this floor sparkling in no time.'

'You're very kind, Griselda,' said Mrs Rubadub. 'Here, take my pink flowery overall so that you don't get yourself all messy. And take my pink flowery scarf to tie up your hair.'

Griselda put on the overall.

'Here, don't shut me in,' yelled Samuel, leaping out of her T-shirt pocket and up onto her head.

Then Griselda put on the headscarf.

'Here, don't tie me down,' yelled Samuel, sliding down a strand of hair and

onto her shoulder. It was then he noticed
something perched on top of Mrs Rubadub's white curls. Griselda had noticed
too. It was Mrs Rubadub's glasses.

'Oh, Griselda, how clever of you to find
them,' said Mrs Rubadub, parking them

54

on the end of her nose. 'That's much better. Now I can see to get on with my spring-cleaning. You can give me back my overall and scarf now.'

'But don't you want any help?' asked Griselda.

Mrs Rubadub looked at the kitchen floor covered in sticky dough and flour.

'Er . . . no thank you,' she said. 'I really think you've helped me enough for one day. Finding my glasses is the best help I could have had.'

Griselda beamed, and she was so

pleased at how well everything had turned out that she decided to try the magic words that would whizz her safely through her garden hedge.

ROSES ARE RED

VIOLETS ARE BLUE

YOOHOO GARDEN HEDGE

I'M COMING THROUGH

Griselda and Samuel whizzed off with a *WHISH*, a *WHOOSH* and a *WHIRL* and a *RRRRRRRIIIIIIPPPPPP* . . . They were back in the cottage, but Griselda's best blue jeans now had a large tear right down the left leg.

'That's positively, absolutely, definitely not supposed to happen, Samuel,' she said. 'I wonder what I'm doing wrong . . . I'll have to try to sew up this tear tomorrow, but now I've run out of white shoe-laces. I'll just have to use some brown hairy string instead.'

5 Griselda and the Village Concert

Griselda, the fairy-godmother, was standing on her right foot with her left foot up on the kitchen table trying to mend the large tear in the left leg of her best pair of blue jeans. It wasn't easy. The brown hairy string she was using kept getting into knots.

'Do you think my jeans will hold together long enough for me to afford a new pair, Samuel?' she asked her multi-coloured mouse.

But Samuel wasn't listening, and snored loudly in reply. He was fast asleep inside Griselda's red winter woolly hat, which was hanging from a peg on the back of the kitchen door.

Just then, the alarm on Griselda's

micro-chipped and scratched super fairy-
godmother watch said, AT THE THIRD
STROKE IT WILL BE THIRTEEN FORTY-TWO
AND AN EXTRA BIT. PRECISELY. Griselda
banged the watch off the table so it went
BLEEP BLEEP.

'Ah,' she said. 'Time to look through
the magic window, and see who needs my
help today.'

Samuel immediately wakened up, and
leapt out of the woolly hat. He liked looking through the magic window. He ran up
Griselda's arm and onto her shoulder.

Griselda went over to the cottage
window. It was divided into six panes of
glass, five clear and one cloudy. Griselda
blew gently on the cloudy pane, then
rubbed it with her sleeve. Slowly a picture began to appear . . .

'Why it's little Harmony Honeysuckle,' said Griselda. 'She's singing in

the concert in the village hall tonight. I wonder why she needs my help today.'

Little Harmony Honeysuckle was sitting on the end of her bed practising her scales. *Doh Re Me Fah Squeak Squeak Te Doh. Doh Te Squeak Squeak Fah Me Re Squeak.* Then she tried her song for the concert. *Squeak the Magic Dragon Squeaked by the Squeak.*

'Oh dear, dear,' said Griselda, sucking in her cheeks and shaking her head. 'What a terrible noise. That'll never do for the concert tonight. I think I'd better whizz off to Harmony's house and help right away. Are you coming, Samuel?'

Samuel blew out his cheeks and nodded his head.

'I'd better come and make sure you don't have any narrow squeaks,' he said. Then he grabbed a strand of Griselda's long fair hair, swung on the end of it, and plopped into the pocket of her T-shirt. The pocket was the safest place to be when whizzing about with Griselda.

While Samuel held on tight, and prepared for take-off, Griselda did a little disco dance on the carpet, then said the magic words: TIME TO BE OFF TO HARMONY'S HOUSE. And they were off, whizzing through the air with a *WHISH*, a *WHOOSH* and a *WHIRL*.

And before you could say SQUEAKY OLD SONGS they had landed in Harmony's

cottage. In Harmony's bedroom. In Harmony's bed.

'Oops sorry, everyone,' said Griselda,

getting tangled up in the duvet. 'I'm not very good at landings.'

'If I had a penny for every time you've said that,' said Samuel, 'I'd be a millionaire mouse.'

But Harmony was delighted to see them.

'It's Griselda and Samuel, Mum,' she said to Mrs Honeysuckle who'd come in from the kitchen to see what all the noise was about.

'Hullo, Griselda,' said Mrs Honeysuckle. 'I didn't see you arrive. Have you come to help Harmony's voice? We've tried everything, but it's no use. Every so often her voice just gives a squeak. I think she's been practising too hard. Maybe she'll have to pull out of the concert tonight.'

'Oh no, Mum,' wailed Harmony. 'I've been looking forward to the concert for ages.'

'Don't worry, Harmony,' said Griselda. 'I'll get your proper voice back for you. First though, I'll do a little spell and remake your bed.' And before anyone could stop her she did a little disco dance on the carpet, closed her eyes and said the magic words.

ROSES ARE RED

VIOLETS ARE BLUE

MAKE UP A BED

AS GOOD AS NEW.

Suddenly there was a *FIZZ*, a *THUMP*, a *BANG* and a great deal of sawing, and they were all squashed into a corner as a brand new bed appeared in the bedroom.

'Oh no,' said Griselda, sitting down on it.

'Oh yes,' said Harmony, bouncing up on it.

'Zzzzzzz,' snored Samuel, giving the

bed a test sleep.

But Mrs Honeysuckle just laughed. 'We'll put the bed into the raffle at the concert tonight,' she said. 'Complete with mouse.'

But Samuel wakened up, and popped back into Griselda's T-shirt pocket. The new bed wasn't as comfortable for sleeping in as an old slipper, a kettle, a fruit bowl, a biscuit tin or a winter woolly hat.

Then Griselda said. 'Now to work on your squeaky voice, Harmony. I'll have it fixed in no time.'

But she didn't. The first spell changed the squeak into a miaow. The second spell changed the miaow into a bark. And the third spell changed the bark back into a squeak again.

Then Griselda had an idea. She whispered it to Samuel, who whispered it to Harmony.

'Great idea, Griselda,' said Harmony.

'Aren't you going to whisper the idea to me,' asked Mrs Honeysuckle.

'Nope,' grinned Harmony. 'It's a secret. You'll hear it at the concert, tonight.'

That night, at the concert in the village hall, Mrs Honeysuckle kept a seat beside her for Griselda and Samuel and they watched and clapped as all the village children came on one by one and sang a song or did a dance.

'I wish I could dance like that,' said Griselda. 'No matter how hard I practise I'm still not very good.'

'At least it's better than your singing,' muttered Samuel.

Then it was Harmony's turn. She came out onto the platform with a big bow on her frilly pink dress, a big bow in her curly black hair, and a big smile on her shiny brown face. She saw her mum and Griselda and Samuel and gave them a little wave. They all gave her a little wave back, except for Samuel who gave her a big wave back, and fell out of the T-shirt pocket into Griselda's bag of jelly babies. But he didn't mind. He was very fond of jelly babies.

Then Harmony began to sing, not *Puff the Magic Dragon* as she was supposed to, but *Three Blind Mice*. She sang . . . *Three squeak Blind squeak Mice . . . Three squeak Blind squeak Mice . . . See squeak How They Run, squeak squeak . . . See squeak How They Run squeak squeak . . .* And the

audience laughed and laughed. They all thought it was a great joke. They didn't know Harmony couldn't help it. Everybody clapped and clapped and Harmony got the biggest cheer of the evening. She gave a little curtsey to the audience, a big grin to her mum, and an enormous wink to Griselda.

And Griselda was so pleased at how well her idea had worked out that she decided to try the magic words again that would whizz her safely through her garden hedge. Samuel crouched down in her pocket, closed his eyes and covered his head with his claws.

ROSES ARE RED

VIOLETS ARE BLUE

THIS IS IT GARDEN HEDGE

I'M COMING THROUGH.

Griselda and Samuel whizzed off with a *WHISH*, a *WHOOSH*, a *WHIRL* and

a *RRRRRRIIIIIIIPPPPP* . . . They were back in the cottage, but Griselda's best pair of blue jeans now had a large tear down the right leg.

'That's positively, absolutely, definitely, certainly not supposed to happen, Samuel,' she said. 'I wonder what I'm doing wrong . . . I'll have to try to sew up this tear tomorrow, but now I've run out of brown hairy string. I'll just have to use my best tartan ribbon instead.'

6   Griselda and the Clothes Designer

Griselda, the fairy-godmother, was sitting on a chair with both feet up on the table, trying to fix the tear in the left leg of her best pair of blue jeans. She had to make big holes down the leg to poke the tartan ribbon through.

'I really think I'll have to empty my piggy-bank, and buy a new pair of jeans,' she said to Samuel, her multi-coloured mouse. 'What do you think?'

But Samuel didn't think anything. He was fast asleep. A loud piercing whistle came from Griselda's new whistling kettle. Samuel was inside. Snoring.

Griselda sighed. 'I don't know why that mouse can't sleep in a mousehole like other mice,' she said.

Just then, the alarm on Griselda's micro-chipped and scratched super fairy-godmother watch said WAKEY WAKEY. Griselda took the watch off, and shook it till it rattled. Then it went BLEEP BLEEP.

'Ah,' she said. 'Time to look through the magic window, and see who needs my help today.'

Samuel immediately wakened up. He liked looking through the magic window. He ran up Griselda's arm and onto her shoulder.

Griselda went over to the cottage window. It was divided into six panes of glass, five clear and one cloudy. Griselda blew gently on the cloudy one, then rubbed it with her sleeve. Slowly a picture began to appear . . .

'Why it's Jeanie McPherson, the famous clothes designer,' said Griselda. 'I wonder why she needs my help today.'

Jeanie McPherson was sitting at her drawing-board surrounded by piles and piles of crumpled paper. She drew dresses then crumpled them up. She drew trousers then crumpled them up. She even drew socks then crumpled them up.

'Squiggles and squares,' she said. 'I haven't had a single good idea, today.

Maybe I should just give up being a famous clothes designer.'

'Oh dear, dear,' said Griselda, sucking in her cheeks and shaking her head. 'What a shame. I think I'd better whizz over to Jeanie's studio right away, and see if I can help. Are you coming, Samuel?'

Samuel blew out his cheeks and nodded his head. 'I'd better come and keep an eye on you,' he said. 'Or better still, two eyes.' Then he grabbed a strand of Griselda's long fair hair, swung on the end of it, and plopped into the pocket of her T-shirt. The pocket was the safest place to be when whizzing about with Griselda.

While Samuel held on tight, and prepared himself for take-off, Griselda did a little disco dance on the carpet, then said the magic words: TIME TO BE OFF TO THE STUDIO. And they were off, whizzing through the air with a *WHISH*, a *WHOOSH* and a *WHIRL*.

And before you could say DOTTY OLD DESIGNS, they had landed in Jeanie McPherson's studio. In the middle of the drawing-board. In the middle of a drawing of a large hat.

'Oops sorry, everyone,' said Griselda, leaving trainer marks round the brim of the hat. 'I'm not very good at landings.'

'You can say that again,' said Samuel.

'I'm not very good at landings,' said Griselda.

'Greetings, Griselda. Put it there, Samuel,' said Jeanie, shaking hands. 'I'm not very good at drawings today either. I can't seem to get anything right, and I've got Mr Bigg, a very important customer, coming at any minute and I've got nothing to show him. What am I going to do?'

'Don't worry, Jeanie,' said Griselda. 'I'm here to help you.'

'I think you should worry, Jeanie,' muttered Samuel. 'Quite a bit.'

'First of all,' said Griselda. 'I'll do a little spell and clean up that drawing I messed up.'

And before anyone could stop her, she did a little disco dance on the carpet and said the magic words.

ROSES ARE RED

VIOLETS ARE BLUE

THE HAT THAT'S ALL MESSY

PLEASE MAKE IT NEW.

There was a *FIZZ*, a *THUMP* and a *BANG*, and Jeanie's studio was immediately covered in hats of every kind. Tall hats, small hats, hats made of wool, hats made for school, hats made in Spain, hats

made for rain, hats made for big heads, hats made for small heads, but not small enough for Samuel who kept trying them on, and disappearing underneath. Finally Jeanie gave him her knitted egg cosy to wear, and that kept him happy.

'I'm sorry about all these hats, Jeanie,' said Griselda. 'Shall I magic them away?'

'No, leave them,' said Jeanie who was worried about what she might get in their place.

Just then there was a ring at Jeanie's front door bell.

'Oh no,' said Jeanie. 'It's Mr Bigg, and I've no designs to show him.

'We could show him my new hat,' said Samuel.

'Don't worry, Jeanie,' said Griselda. 'I'll think of something.' And she waded through the hats to the front door to let the important customer in.

'Come in, Mr Bigg important customer,' she said. 'My name's Griselda. Mind the hats.'

Then Samuel leapt onto Mr Bigg's shoulder. 'I'm Samuel,' he said, 'the multi-coloured mouse, and this is my multi-coloured hat which keeps my multi-coloured head warm, and will be a useful way of carrying my jelly babies because mice don't have pockets.'

Jeanie groaned and covered her face, but Mr Bigg just laughed out loud.

'Jeanie,' he said. 'You're a genius.

Where did you get two such marvellous models? And look at what they're wearing. The multi-coloured mouse hat is superb. I will make the design up in every shape and size. I can see by all these hats how long it's taken you to come up with the right one. And Griselda's jeans really are fantastic. What a design. They're so terribly tattered, so beautifully battered, so absolutely awful . . . I will make the design up, and call it the new scarecrow look.'

'Scarecrow look,' squeaked Griselda.

'Yes,' said Mr Bigg. 'By this time next week it will be the latest fashion.'

'But . . .' said Jeanie.

'But but . . .' said Griselda.

'Thank you very much,' said Samuel, when Mr Bigg opened his wallet, and handed them over a large pile of money before he left.

And Griselda was so pleased at how well everything had turned out that she said. 'I think I'll try that spell again to whizz us safely through the garden hedge.'

But Samuel, counting up their share of the money, this time managed to stop her. 'Oh no you don't,' he said.

'Why not?' asked Griselda.

'Because,' said Samuel. 'With this money from Mr Bigg we can forget all about that SILLY OLD SPELL and buy a gate!'